# I Was Never In A Position To Survive Tertiary

# Are You Ready…?

MBALI MLABA

Pharos Books

**ISBN: 978-93-5546-127-8**
**eISBN: 978-93-5546-128-5**



**Publisher: Pharos Books (P) Ltd.**
Plot No.-55, Main Mother Dairy Road
Pandav Nagar, East Delhi-110092
**Phone**: 011-40395855, +14049995474
**WhatsApp:** +91 8368220032
**E-mail**: sales@pharosbooks.in
**Website**: www.pharosbooks.in
**Edition:** 2022

**Printed By:** Sushma Book Binding House, Okhla Industrial Area, Phase II, New Delhi-110020

**I Was Never In A Position To Survive Tertiary**
**Are You Ready…?**
**MBALI MLABA**

# Contents

# Summary

It is always difficult for parents or for your family to accept the fact that now you are going to start a new life, where they won't be around to look after you every now and then like they used to. One of the things they do before you leave them for the tertiary level is that they make sure to talk to you about how you should behave and what you should do and what you should not do. They give you the best advice on how you should take care of yourself. Always remember the things you were told by your parents or your family. The advice and lessons they gave you are going to see you through all those years you are going to spend till you finish your diploma or degree level. When you enter the university, you are going to there to represent your family, their values and make them proud. Remember who you are, what you want and the most important thing what is the purpose of why you are at the university.

> **NB**: *Remember, you are not going there to impress your peers or just to fit in. It is okay to being real with yourself than faking the true person you are for other people you are going to meet there. Your happiness comes first. It's all about staying true to yourself and know yourself, and understand the person you are. Set yourself goals and wake up every day and work towards achieving whatever goal you set for yourself.*

# Introduction

All of us have an idea of living without our parents and family. We all wish to be on our own, and take decisions of our own, but how many of you talk about how difficult it is to be without your family or an elder who will tell you what is right and what is wrong because most of us use the freedom in a most inappropriate way where we even forget the main aim of why we are at the university, what is expected from us and what we should do. We tend to change and forget the most important things by ending up bringing shame to our parents and family. We tend to change the way we were raised in our family because we are no longer showing the reflection of the respect and lessons we were told. For example, by lying because we want to make ourselves feel important in the presence of our friends by showing off, forgetting how hard some of our parents or our guardians are working hard for that money. This book is entailed more about such things that are happening at the university rather than what you should not do as a person who is about to enter the university or already at the university.

## Chapter 1

# How is it akin to live with no parents/family?

At first, you enjoy the freedom of not being watched by your family members or your parents. You get used to it, you adapt to the surroundings as time goes by that you are finally all alone, and some find the right to take whatever verdict they want about their life, because they know nobody is there to tell them that they are wrong. It's all up to you as an individual to do what you want.

Many tend to behave in a very inappropriate way not thinking about what tomorrow will bring, as much as you will have that freedom at a tertiary level, but make sure you play prudent that you not going to change because of this phase of the university that you are facing. To tell the truth, the university phase will pass and then what will happen to you.

I'm pretty sure you don't want to be someone who laments things he/she has done because of failing to face that university phase, and also you don't want to be an individual who will get sick after finishing his/her studies and end up not enjoying the money you worked hard for but if you can change and have good intentions about yourself and your future.

This is how life is like when you live without your parents. You don't get someone who will walk with you all the way through the process of growing up. You do things on your own, not even sure if you are still doing it the right way. At some point in your life you may fail and do things you never expected to do, but make sure when you fail you accept to yourself that you did wrong, and find ways which can help you in revealing a true definition of yourself. This may seem easy but when you are facing this genuinely, it is not really easy but difficult to deal with.

Living without your parents requires you to learn to position yourselves by taking good decisions, and remaining the person you are and your worth, not allowing the peer pressure to control but learn to control whatever obstacle you will deal with it in a good way. To your peers you may seem an idiot, but today I am telling you that you are not, and you will never be if you were able to master these things, I mentioned above.

The things that will happen is that the very same people who never took you seriously or looked at you as a dupe will come running for advice to you. Give them, show them the real you and let them see it. Stay true to yourself, and do not allow other people of your age to take you in a wrong direction. Learn to speak up and embrace yourself. You will be astonished to find that you will meet people like you, and that you can change them and they will learn from you.

Inasmuch as we have all the freedom we want when we enter the tertiary level and have an opportunity to be at the residence. I suggest we use the freedom wisely and not to think about what is happening now, but consider looking backwards to where you come from and why you wanted to pursue that qualification you are doing. There is nothing more consequential than a person who makes sure they do not change from what they have been raised to, and where people who always bear that in their mind, I believe they succeed in life. My opinion is to encourage each and every one to never forget your background, religion, respect, and discipline that you have been taught at home by mistake, and to use that freedom when you are no longer staying with your family wisely. Know who you are, where you are going, the reason why you are at the tertiary, and put your family first and not your friends.

## Chapter 2

# Stages you face

As we grow up, we face stages that are part of growing up and making us know the difference between identifying, the wrong and the right. For example, adolescence is a stage that both male and female face to reach that stage. Just like when you are about to enter the university, it is a stage of maturity, because now your parents or family have trusted you enough to let you go to the university and stay there without them.

Sometimes, we think we have grown up enough to take our own decisions without consulting our parents or an elderly such as our sisters or brothers, or people who can help, because they have already passed the stage an individual is facing. We decide not to involve anybody that is why if we continue like this we are going to find ourselves in big trouble.

If you end up not having someone to call, you will live with regrets, which may lead to a stress that is not necessary. Today, I am telling you that in every stage of your life, it is important to have someone you trust, someone you can rely on, and someone you know can give best advice.

A person may ask why I am saying this, it is because you cannot take decisions yourself and you can be wrong sometimes. You may think you are taking the right decision when you are not, but if you had someone to tell that this is the right decision, you probably could have taken the right decision. I can tell whether it's a good decision or not, and if not why? Make sure you do not find someone of your age, because sometimes you two may think you are doing what is right, when you are not doing right at all. But if you had someone a little bit older, than that person will never lie to you. Remember, I said someone you can trust and that individual you must be sure, he/she will never lie to you. It could be anyone as long as you trust that individual e.g., your family, relative, and friend, etc.

As stages are part of our growing process, we can never dodge it, or take a step forward without having to face every stage in life. When you are at the tertiary level, I advise that you learn to speak up, because some of us are not used to talking. They like keeping things to themselves even when they are facing challenges and when it's time to take decisions, because decision is a part of our life journey.

I'm saying this because when you grow up, you need to take decisions concerning your life about what you want, and what you are deciding to do with your life. As you are in the tertiary level, you will have to decide what life you are choosing to live? So that is why it is very important to speak up with those we trust, when you are taking some decisions in your life. Sometimes, they help you to grow as an individual. I feel it is like preparing you to learn to take good decisions for yourself.

## Chapter 3

# Where are you going with your life…?

You need to develop this question within you, and ask yourself where exactly I am going with my life. What is it that, I want with my life and what is it that I am doing, that shows I am working towards achieving the life that I want?

You know that by asking yourself these kind questions, firstly you will retain information who you are and where you are going, and I believe these questions will remind you as an individual of the important things, we tend to forget when we are in the university, which is your Background.

Someone may inquire what she is trying to say, or did she forget her background when she was in the university, and my answer to that is, 'YES' as of the life. I was living when I was in the university, which was not like the one I was living at home. You know, at times I would develop questions within me like Mbali, who are you? You were not raised like this, and you've never done this all your life, is this the life you want to live from now onwards?

Well, I never dealt the right way with these questions. I was denying the information and I tried being someone I was not. Sometimes I thought this would lead me to depression, because I was not at peace with myself. These questions kept coming every time I was alone. I was successively away from the reality, and the only thing which was keeping me away from these questions was not being unaided or being around people or someone. There's nothing agonizing from pretending to being someone, you are not and from running away from the reality of who you are.

You are insincere to yourself and not to people, when you begin having these questions that are not there for you, because they don't know that all this will hunt you alone, and you will be left by yourself regretting everything of which is something. I don't want other people to experience that some of us are not strong, they are fragile in a way that they will see suicide as a good choice , which is something I never thought about, but all I have to write is so that people will learn and know that they can survive this life . You can survive everything that life throws at you. It is possible and I believe each and every one of you can.

***In my own view,** as **a person it is important not to forget your background, because that's what keeps you going in being something you want to become, because when you look back you will be exactly like what you wanted to become. I don't want to be determined by where I am coming from, but where I am going. Your parents might have failed somewhere and were not able to give you what you wanted, but do you know that you can give them the life, they also wished to live, and you will give your children what your parents were not able to give you; since you know how difficult it was, and you don't wish that for your children.***

To sum up, what I have learned as I grow up in life is that, you have to fight by working hard, and prove yourself of what you are capable of doing in order to get rewards at the end. Yes, you will face obstacles and challenges along the way, but let me tell you that you have the power in you to face those challenges and obstacles. Don't ever give up, but keep on fighting because you know where you are going, and you know which life you want to live in the next coming years, so don't be moved by diminutive things and whatever challenges you might come across as you grow up.

Don't be moved by some subjects and don't allow those subjects to stand in your way and to have power over you. Change your approach if it means that. Another thing which kills us in the university, is the lecture of that module, how you are expecting to pass that module and when you are not making the grade; you will blame that lecture change and in order to succeed in life, do not carry on with that approach for you will not get anywhere with it.

One more thing you must bear in mind that in order to succeed at some point in your life, you will fail and when you fail you may feel like that was the end of your life. Please allow me to tell you that Failure is a part of the process in order to succeed as when you fail you learn, you will in no way repeat that mistake. There's nothing good like failing forward because failing backwards, remembering your weak spots and what people are saying, concerning you yes, they will talk and giggle but keep on moving forward.

One must always develop this question within themselves to show that you are not just living the life, and that you are not just studying because you have to impress your family. This one is for you to show that you have a direction about your life, you know where you are going from, and you are planning for your future. This one will also be seen by getting that diploma or degree in time if you haven't got it, it is also not a problem. You can also understand that we have different journeys to walk alone, not with our friends or family, but the journey is for you to walk alone.

Chapter 4

# The freedom and decision-making

Once we finish High School, we all can't wait to go to the university because we desire the freedom of being away from our parents to do everything, we have been longing for all these past years and to actually experience the life without them, and the irritation of being told what and what not to do. There's one thing that our parents do not understand that they are trying to protect us, whereas on the other side, we want to experience life in our own way and to make bad decisions that will teach us in order for us to learn, but our parents are always there trying to prevent us not to do the mistakes that they have done.

According to me, the only way for us to learn is when we take our own decisions good or bad, but in the end, they teach us how to learn life. Inasmuch as our parents are always there wanting to be involved in everything we do; we are not going to grow, and we will not experience life.

What will happen is that we will learn that things are done for us, and we don't have to do anything. That kills us, because there are times where our parents are not there, and we have to do things in our own way, but we can't do, because we expect our parents to do it for us. This comes with decision-making, our parents need to teach us to take wise decisions and not to take decisions on our behalf, because that's what kills lots of students when they enter the tertiary level, and they have to decide without their parents.

Don't get confused. I was stating the facts that our parents are doing without the knowledge, I have just shared above. I am not meaning we should not listen to our parents, we should, but at the same time try to take wise decisions for yourself. You will need your parents to be involved, and that is why it is a must that we learn from our decisions that our parents are trying to protect us from repeating the same mistakes that our parents have done, when they were growing up, because that is their main aim, they are trying by all means to protect us. All we need to do is to listen to them, and the most important thing to learn is to take wise decisions for ourselves that will help us to learn not to allow our parents to take decisions for us, because some decisions we take in life does not need our parents, but needs the wisdom we learned from our parents. I hope you get it right.

We all have that state of mind because we don't know the challenges, we may face and decisions we may take without the approval of our parents. We feel like our parents are taking wrong decisions for us and don't want us; because we want to behave the way we like and take our decisions, but how many of you have ever asked themselves if our parents can take bad decision for us, because they want to satisfy their needs through us.

The answer is that our parents have all the information about life that we don't have, and they try by all means to protect us from taking wrong decisions, they guide us to each and every step and even though when we grow up and reach a certain level of age we think, we are smarter than our parents which is so wrong. We need to listen to them and also learn to take good decisions in our way.

This is the life we always wanted, having the freedom, but let me tell you it is important that you behave in the same way, you would have behaved even when your parents were not around; because you are not doing them a favour. But, you are helping yourself to represent them exactly in the same way they raised you to be and always retained information that your parents have reached the stages you are in and you are about to face, so ask and tell them whenever you are taking a decision or, have someone who's older than you to speak to because there are things sometimes you face in life. You cannot tell your parents in case you have a decision to take in that kind of a situation, or who will tell you the truth in order for you to grow. And, that will teach you to take wise decisions instead of taking whatever decision you feel is right at that time and end up regretting, because you were not speaking, or asking for help and that is not something I want, and I wish for people who are following. I hope, you will take a lesson from here and apply it to yourself.

When you enter the university, you have all the freedom you always wanted, and it's up to you how you are going to use it in a fruitful way or in a way where you will not represent where you come. This is where you decide what you should do, but what I want to tell you is that **do not allow the environment to change you, not even your friends may change you. Always keep in mind the reason you are in the university, and never forget but keep working towards the reason you are in the university so you will succeed.**

> ***In my own view, take a decision that will make you happy and it is something you want rather than taking a decision to please your peers, because you will never be happy and you will have regrets, because you never put yourself first to do what will make you happy as much as you have the freedom, so make sure you use it wise.***

Lastly, do not use the freedom in a way where you find yourself taking a last minute decision without having to think through the decision you want to take. You don't want to regret because of the decisions you took without having to think, and never let your close friends decide for you. You have the power to decide for yourself, because bear in mind that a friend may lead you to a wrong direction. Another thing you must keep in mind in your life is that you will meet temporary people, so be able to identify a person you meet for a reason and the temporary ones. The ones you meet for a reason is there to stay, it's okay to ask a friend about the decisions you want to take; but be wise which ones you are talking to. Not every friend will wish you all the success, some people you will meet are there to make sure they bring you down.

## Chapter 5

# Residence Life

Residence life is different from home, so keep that in mind. While staying in a residence, you will be doing everything for yourself without being helped as you used to at home. For example, things like cooking, washing, cleaning your room, buying your own grocery and so on.

It is important that you practice these things mentioned above, so that you can adapt easily at the university. Some students find it very difficult to adapt, because of the things they did not practice, while they were still living with their parents at home and now, that they are on themselves, it becomes a problem.

My advice, especially to those, who have not yet gone into the university is that even though residence life is going to be new and different to you, "***Do not allow the university phase to overpower you, or to control you in a way that you become totally different from the child who was taught very well and disciplined at home.***" Yes, there are times in life where you do a mistake, you never thought you would.

In that case, learn from that mistake and don't blame yourself, as you will end up having regrets. Do not compare the mistake you did with others, because you won't find happiness, but you will have regrets. Understand this, people don't make the same mistakes, even friends, siblings no matter what the case may be, and you know why. Because, we never plan for mistakes to happen, we don't ask for them to happen, it just happens in an instant. In most cases, it makes us learn to become successful people and in order for them and you to reach a certain level, and they will make the same mistakes just like any of us does, because mistakes are a way for us to learn. Without mistakes, we are not getting anywhere. You know what that means…it means we won't learn unless you learn from your experience, because you never want to repeat the same mistakes, and the question is that how many of us are learning through mistakes that we sometimes make in life. Mistakes can be the decisions we took lightly, it can be anything that you never planned on doing.

In addition, residence life is where you have all the freedom you want, it is up to you how you use the freedom you have and that depends on how you were raised, but sometimes as a person you get distracted… what do I mean by this... are you wondering what am I going to say… listen, I mean when a person gets distracted is when he/she behaves not in the same way as they were raised, or disciplined at home. They are using this freedom of being with their peers in a most inappropriate way, that you can't even think even their family may hear ormight get disappointed. They tend to take the decision according to what their peers may want, not what they really want…I want to tell you something very important, your dignity is everything, it identifies the person you are, whether you are a girl or a boy and another thing, I want to touch on in terms of dignity is that you must bear in mind that boys dignity is not for women at all… how are you going to make a great brother, uncle, father if you don't respect your dignity, how will you expect children, sisters and others if you don't respect your dignity? Dignity is for both men and women to respect.

Lastly, in my own view….do not let a friend or anyone to decide for you because you might meet some peers, who does nothing for you and tell you. Your parents are not here, so decide for yourself and do what makes you comfortable to do. ***In my own view, do not go with the crowd, you will lose the life you want, and the person you want to be and it's difficult to leave them, because you have been doing things together and take another path. By taking another path and leaving them, you will get criticism from them.***

## Chapter 6

# A Graduate Student

Not everything is appalling and you should be warned about it when you enter the university. You go to the university or college with the aim of going forward with your career, because you want to pursue and make your family swollen with pride, because most of our parents never had an opportunity to go into the universities or colleges as us. Each and every one of us don't want to stay unqualified just like our parents which is why we go to the universities and colleges to get education, which will qualify us to our job description we want and careers we desire to pursue.

***In my own view, most of the students when they go into the universities and colleges get disrupted by the life which is new to them. We all benefit from the freedom we tend to have when we enter the university. You are also going to experience that freedom, but I am also asking every individual that even if you have the freedom never forget the reason why you are at the university or may be a college, FET and other institutions.***

Another thing, I want to mention about the tertiary level is that you don't only learn based on the qualification you applied for, but you learn even beyond that because that is where you meet different people. In most cases, you work in groups with people where you discover yourself or if you are a person who knows how to work with others or learn with others in a study group. In terms of working with groups, there are difficult times where you learn how are other people behaving. When it comes in doing work, you learn how to deal with those situations and that actually prepares you for work, because you will also meet the people you do not know, and you will have to work with them too. You will also learn in terms of life, you will grow, you will also learn other skills, and you will learn more about politics. There's this mentality that is known …the one we grow up thinking that you have an idea of it. I know you are already thinking of one, oh yes! that we grow up knowing politics is for old people and we exclude ourselves, but when you enter the college or university you will then know the importance of politics in the country, we live in.

Most of us grow up without knowing the significance of politics as those things were far from us and that is why you find it very difficult. Some of the students participate to get involved, because it's not something we were once told of. We tend to ask questions like, why is it important for me to know it because in an environment you grow up in, "politics was for old people," and if you ever mention the political party you are in that is war with some people who were never a part of the political party.

> ***In my own view, as we grow up the system or the way things are done are changing, we are moving with times. Nowadays for you to get a job you must have a background of the political party that you are. Isn't that new. Think about it, well. I know there are still communities where you don't get to feel free with the political party you are supporting, but that must not be a reason for you to not move with the times, because you might have a problem when you graduate and it's time for you to go looking for a job.***

Someone might develop a question "is this writer into politics. Why is she even mentioning politics?" The answer is that there are things in life we may not want to be a part of, but that thing is a way for us to get where we want to be. We definitely have to do it. Even if we are not active, as long as you have a good background they want you to get on with your dreams based on the qualifications you are studying.

Moving on, tertiary education gives us the life we prayed for. We always wanted the life we dreamt of when we grew up. Tertiary education prepares us for the qualification we are doing or about to do. It propels us to every area of the work we will be doing when we get into the industry. It gives us more knowledge and how we should go about doing the work by teaching us practically the areas which fall under our qualifications.

A graduated student is you... I mean you. I am curious wondering who were you thinking of. I am referring to weren't you thinking of an individual who has already graduated? A big YES and let me remind you that when you go into the tertiary level you already have an idea at the back of your mind that at some point in your life you will graduate and make your family proud of you.

A definition of a graduated student is one who finishes all the subject required to do as per the qualification level plus an in-service training. If the qualification requires a training then it is a must for a student in order to graduate, but there are qualifications with no training which is needed in order for them to graduate.

Have you ever imagined yourself graduating and coming back home with a certificate either of a diploma/degree…visualizing and imagination is vital, it tells that a person has a purpose of where they see themselves in the next coming years with their studies and even about your life. Imaginations are powerful.

There's nothing more beautiful than when a student is graduating. It is a big moment for each and every one of us. It matters a lot to your family and to you, this is where you pave the way to great things for which you are meant, or this is where you should grab every opportunity that may come your way with both hands, and use it wisely.

It doesn't matter when you are graduating, since you are not in a competition with someone else. What matters the most is that at the end you will also be a graduate, no matter what may stand in your way in trying to stop you, but keep moving forward. Learn to do your things without involving people, because in life we sometimes meet people who just want to discourage, and prevent us from where we are going with our lives, that is why it is very important to know your circle since everyone is not your friend, and there is no one to help you grow. Some people out there are like parasites, they come to get what they want, or what they will benefit from and leave you like that. I'm sure you don't want that for yourself, that is why you need to read, what the writer is telling you in order to be aware of such people in your life.

***In my own view, what I have learned from seeing things is that some graduates don't apply for jobs that offer low income and low positions. Most of us are rushing for big positions in order to apply. That is wrong. You don't start from a big position, but you start from a low position. Slowly, you will learn and you will show them what are you capable of within the position you are in, for they are the ones who will choose for you for a bigger position.***

This one is very consequential if you look into the many advertised posts for graduate students or people. If you would notice, many posts want 3 years' experience. What do you understand by that? According to you, what do you think is best for you to do, or how should government deal with this situation, because the fact is that we have just graduated, and where are we going to get the 3 years' experience?

Let me tell you what I think. Nowadays, we have in-service training, and the internship program which is for 24 months which makes 2 years. You already have 2 years' experience plus a 3-6 months experience from the in-service training. My point is let's involve ourselves, let's move, let's go out there and try to do something, which will work best for us, because we do not have the power to tell the government our views, but rather than staying and doing nothing, let's avoid developing such habit. Yes, we are going to study but without an experience we cannot go forward. At least try to do something wisely and decide for your future. You are not going to succeed in the corner, but when you go out involving yourself, something might work out for you. I know there is a course in the tertiary level that does not need WIL (Work Integrated Learning), but as a student when you are done with your exams at the end of the year, go and ask for participation in the government department, private companies and so on where you can work. Let's also work with the government since all post requires a minimum 3 years' experience. Talking about this and how government should make things will not happen because this system is not going to change, because you have a qualification, it has been there so at least try to meet it with everything we could do. Talking is not helping but action does make a way forward and you are not going to regret yourself about taking action in my opinion.

In conclusion, I encourage that it is better you get unemployed with something in hand than be without something that you are not proud of. We get lots of discouragement from people who are not studying because when we get unemployed, we return to our homes. Remember, our time is not the same after graduating, some may find a job and others may not, but that doesn't mean your time will never come. You don't know what God is preparing you for and what God is teaching us. We all need to be patient and don't want to do things the people in the university are doing. It is okay to be different, so trust your journey and keep on pushing. If it means you have to apply 15 times then do it and don't give up, because perhaps that God was testing you to see if you are patient or not so keep having trust on God. And, do not let your journey be distracted by small things that may try to come and steal your focus or change your perspective. Never allow that and be aware of such kind of people in your life.

Chapter 7

# Fear of Failure

We all have fear of failure, depending on which area a person is fearing to fail. We develop questions within us for example, the writer once developed a question on what will I do if I fail? With a negative mind I gave the answer or a conclusion of what will be the end of me if I fail. The second question was, what people will say if I fail. I myself will feel embarrassed that goes in hand with developing a low self-esteem. These were the questions, I asked myself with the thought of if I were to fail, how would I deal with failure. Let's look at fear of failure in learning, which goes hand in hand with fear of failure in general in every area of your life, where you face difficulties or challenges with regards to fear of failure. Before getting on fear of failure, I am learning what I am to enlighten to you.

***Do not fear to fail, failure is part of our journey which prepares us to be where we want to be or to be the people, we want to be. It makes us strong to want to go even deeper than we thought, so when you fail in your life do not just sit back and let failure overpower you but rather fight even more. Start over again if it means to come up with a new strategy....***

**YOU ARE MORE POWERFUL THAN FAILURE. FIGHT THE FEAR OF FAILURE WITHIN YOU, BECAUSE YOU WILL FAIL AT SOME POINT IN YOUR LIFE. THAT PART**

**IS EACH AND EVERY ONE OF US. THIS IS TO TELL YOU WHAT TO DO IF YOU FACE FAILURE. GET UP AND DO THE THINGS YOU LIKE TO DO OR YOU HAVE NEVER DONE BEFORE. START OVER AGAIN IF YOU HAVE TO.**

How to fight fear failure? What are you thinking? The answer is the first thing that came up to your mind. In order to fight fear of failure, we need to develop a positive mind and a positive attitude towards the things we face, as fear of failure is one of them. What do I mean by that…? I mean you cannot say, you are fighting failure when you have a bad attitude and negative mind. You will have doubts and not be able to take a wise decision in dealing with failure. This will create a problem which will cause you to become stressed. A positive mind and a good attitude is the key to fight back failure and become more powerful.

## Let's get into the fear of failure in learning….

The fear of Failure according to the writer refers to self-doubt that tends to develop in an individual not believing in himself. Even if you work hard, you still have doubt if you will do well or if you look at the top achievers you don't see yourself being one of them, or you feel that you will never be like them. They are talented and wise by nature unlike you who work hard, but still get 60% at the end. Let me tell you, if you believe in yourself, you can trust me and you can work, according to the standards you have set for yourself and not people around you or just people in general.

There are various ways of reading, so find for yourself which one do you fall under and then use the strategy which will work best for you and then study . Teach yourself to read every day even when you are not reading your study materials. Teach your mind to get used to reading so that you won't have a problem when you have to study for your tests or exams.

According to (Covington: 1992), often in response to this fear of failure, students may actively sabotage their chances of success by procrastinating or leaving tasks until the last minute, or expend little effort, so that they have an excuse if they do not do so well. This excuse serves as a protective function in that they can blame their poor performance on their procrastination. Students can be characterized in terms of three typologies: those that are success oriented, those that are failure **avoidant**, and those that are failure accepting. The failure-avoidant students are the classic failure fearers. (Covington, 1992; Martin, 2010; Martin & Marsh, 2003) has separated many failure fearers into two groups: (1) students who deal with their fear of failure by hard work and/or success – referred to as **over strives** or sometimes as **perfectionists**, and (2) students who deal with their fear of failure through counterproductive activity that is aimed more at self-protection than attaining success.

The **over strive** tends to avoid failure by succeeding. The factors that are associated with this form of failure fearing include anxiety, perceptions of low control, and an unstable self-esteem. The risks inherent in this form of failure fearing are two-fold. First, it renders the academic journey as somewhat unpleasant and fraught with anxiety perceptions of low control and unstable self-esteem.

Moreover, when over strives don't succeed, failure is seen as proof of suspected incompetence, which increases the risk of falling into the second and more productive form of failure avoidance.

The **self-protector** does not aim much to avoid failure, but to avoid the implications of failure through strategically manoeuvring ways in order to protect their self-worth. By doing so they are able to mitigate the extent to which failure reflects poorly on their ability and consequent self-worth.

With the above information quoted from Covington, identify which one are you? Are you over strives or self-protector, then from there you should develop a question of how can I overcome it. Now that you know, you are falling under self-protector think of ways you can fight this thing of fearing failure, because this is very important for everyone, and which one you fall under will help you as a person to know the person you are in general. You will never grow if you still fear failure, fight failure and become stronger by what made you fail and be willing to start afresh to fix where you were not doing well.

Accept the fact that you fail in order to move forward and fix your failures, without accepting you will always feel sorry for yourself, and have unnecessary questions which is not really good for your health. Know that failure is part of the journey for us to grow, how you are going to grow if you haven't accepted that you failed and you have to fix your failures where you did not do well as expected. An additional element, do not use failure even on things that you did by choice than deceiving yourself, because within you will know you shouldn't have done like you did and you will have regrets.

To conclude, you know sometimes we fail even when we have tried but we still fail, do you know why. I want to share my story with you. To cut a long story short, I used to think I was working hard when I wasn't. You might be wondering that I used to read a lot, but I was not careful and never focused in class. I told myself, I can read without the clarification of the lecture ohm… well I thought I was wiser than the lecture, but do you know what happened. That semester I did not pass as I expected. I asked myself why is it that I am not doing well even though I studied. This question kept ringing in my mind. I had a one-on-one session with myself, where I realized this thing of not focusing was really killing me. I then started another semester with a new focus. I tried to listen. I studied and then did exceptionally well. Sometimes, all we need is a one-on-one session with ourselves in order to find who we are, where we are lacking and what is it that we are not doing well. I hope this will teach you and help change your perspective.

## Chapter 8

# Change is not easy

It is indeed true that change is not easy from what the writer observed in general. We black people don't want to change from what we know, and we don't want to try new things or learn new languages. We always stick to what we know and that makes it difficult to change. We have learned from our grandparents that when we grow up with that mindset, we thought that was right, because in Zulu they say *INDLELA IBUZWA/IFUNDWA KWABAPHAMBILI.* We all don't want to break that rule because if we do, we are going to find ourselves in trouble which is something we don't want to find ourselves in.

Don't take this for granted because in life you will face a situation, which will require you to change and that will be your only choice in order to move forward with your life, because we can't predict what life will bring to each and every one of us.

The above was about life in general so, let's get back to the main aim of the book ….

Change is not easy even when you enter the university. You have to adapt to a life of doing things on your own; have to cook, clean, wash yourself which some people really find it the most difficult thing to do because they were not doing these things at home. Now, they find it very difficult to buy grocery that needs to last a month, or clean your room. It is not really easy to adapt to all these thing in an instant, if you were not preparing yourself, or if you are not used to doing all of this, I have mentioned. I would like to give a piece of advice to those that are still actually preparing, to go with one of your family members in terms of grocery, so you would learn how to do it yourself.

I know you may feel like you are moving forward when you haven't even been accepted to any tertiary level, so let me tell you to believe in yourself that you will do it. Imaginations are powerful, if you are putting a picture of yourself to where you want to be in the future, you will definitely be there and by also working hard prove to yourself and not to anybody else because that is where people tend to get lost in their direction, to where they are going. You know why because they tend to notice what people will say, if I do this they are tending to prove other people who have no idea, where the individual is aiming to be with his/her life.

Adapting to a new environment is not easy, the fact that you will meet other people and get to know them, when you were used to the people around you…you know sometimes you may even think if we were all born for one thing or you and your friends were born for everything, life will be very easy because you know you will be with them throughout the journey and you were both born for it. The reality is that you have to explore new things you do not know and are not used to, and create new friends for starting a new life. Creating friends is an issue because you do not know the people. You aren't even sure if they are like the ones you will find along the way. They are good or bad for you because you are responsible for your life, and you know what kind of people you want to associate yourself with.

**Note**: We don't go to the same tertiary with our High School friends, since it is very rare to find those friends from the same High School, and still be on the same tertiary with their friends. I was unlikely to find my friend in the same institution I was going to, we didn't plan, I didn't even know she was also going there. We found each other on the registration date. I was very pleased to hear that she is also registering. May be that might happen to you too with one of your friends….

Bear in mind that you might be accepted to another tertiary without your friends, and you have to go there and study. That is how life is changing after High School. Change isn't easy, isn't it?

Before closing, I just want to share my story with the story that might be your story too or is your story/was your story….

**Words are powerful and** you might be wondering why is the writer saying this? What story is the writer talking about? I have learned that the things that we speak about our life are very powerful. So, be warned about what you are speaking about your life, and about your future.

When I remember all the things, I used to say about my life when I was still in High School, those words have turned into reality. Some people might take this for granted, thinking I am just saying you know. You are just saying… honestly, I am not. I used to speak powerful words about my future and some of my siblings would say that I do not know the life you know, and you will fail so don't say those words again. I would just laugh and say within me, that I am going to prove them wrong as they do not know me. I will work hard so I won't fail, and I will do that exactly. I would sometimes count my age and say that at the age of 18, I will be doing my Matric and at the age of 21, I will be done with studies and that's what happened exactly. I finished my diploma at the age of 21 but it wasn't easy, but I was pushing myself to prove that I can do this.

I will not mention everything again. I was only saying that it turns into reality. This is just an overview of a picture to show those who are following me that they can also do it, and those who are above me. Be careful, about what you are saying about your life, not even what you are saying to other people, it might be your siblings, friends, and cousins and so on. Make sure you speak words that will build someone up and create the individual to be the best version of themselves, even when people are not speaking powerful words, but don't return that back.

## Chapter 9

# Tertiary prepares you to grow wise and to work….

The question may pop in your mind how is tertiary preparing me to grow….? Does this mean if I don't go to tertiary, I will not grow? What does the writer mean by saying this…..? These maybe the questions you are asking yourself. Let's breakdown for you to understand what I mean by saying this.

Here's one thing that happens when you are going to the tertiary right…? You are going to live there without your parents and family. You are now all alone, and your parents trust you enough to allow you to go stay at the students' residence, isn't it..? Since you are going to stay without your family, they give you the money to buy food. Now, you don't have to think of clothes only but also of food and other things you will need. How are you going to use that money…? You have to think and decide and allocate yourself a budget that you will need to buy food, isn't it…? Think about how you are going to do this, because when you were at home you have never even bothered to ask about how they are budgeting for grocery. Now, you have to do this. You have no choice or unless you decide to go with other things you will starve. You need to be told about it so that you get used to buying everything yourself all the time. You are learning for example how to use the money, not only that, now you are also learning not to waste money on things that are not useful. Before using your money, the first step is to allocate the money according to your needs. Do you see now how the tertiary is preparing us to grow, because we don't get involved into all these things when we are at home, it is only our parents who are involved but then tertiary teaches us a lot of things that we were not used to doing at our homes?

Now you see we are not going to the university for getting our qualifications that we are pursuing, but we also learn about things in general. Honestly, we have the time to get involved into knowing how money is used or how to plan a budget when buying grocery at home. We don't have time for that but when we enter the university and stay at the student's residence we learn about that and know how to use money.

Furthermore, in my own view, tertiary teaches us to be able to stand for ourselves, it changes our perspective that we can actually survive without being around our family. It creates in our mind that we can bring a life that we have been dreaming of in our families. It gives us an opportunity to prepare while we have the time to be independent in case we lose our parents or family members because that is the reality of life. We also think of that as we grow, because life makes us realize what is more important to do while having time with our parents, so even when they left you, you have something in hand that you have created for yourself and for your future.

Tertiary is basically teaching us to think more about our future and that is where you start thinking about what you want in life and what you are going to create for yourself. It gives us a picture that we should not have hope or trust on our parents or guardians only, because those people are going to leave us at some point of time, and what are we going to do after them since they are our only hope. That is why we go into the tertiary to create our future life. In the tertiary, we learn the reality of life that our family is not telling us about that makes us grow not only by age, but makes us grow with our way of thinking about life. We also grow with the challenges we face in the tertiary plus the mistakes we are making without any knowledge. What I have realized is that we learn nothing when we are at home, we don't learn anything because our parents are covering for us. Sometimes, they accept things with fearing humiliation that we have put them through, but when we are without them we tend to see where we have been wrong, and how we are going to fix those mistakes, we have put ourselves in.

In my opinion, tertiary is not about education only, which is the reason why we go to higher learning education, but also about life in general. As much as we go there for education, but on the other side that is where we learn more about life, that is where we need to take decisions about the life we want to live in the near future. At home, a person may wish to achieve so many things, but have you noticed do they achieve those things by staying at home…?

Not going out there to observe and learn about what they want, my point is that a person just doing nothing and staying at home may wish one thing, but only the one in the tertiary level will get what he/she wants. Because, the one in tertiary has an advantage of opportunity and it is easy to go out there and create waves, but not unless someone at home is working hard to go out there and create waves with people that can help .

**Note**: I am not saying that people who are not into higher institutions can't do anything. It depends on a person how much they are working hard for what they want, because even a tertiary person cannot use the advantage that you have you know.

I remember, when I first attended the first year meeting at our residence, one of the lady who was our Residence Advisor said that we should not focus on the course, we are here to do. I asked myself, why is she saying that it is necessary…? There are so many courses here, and should I find out about all of them, is she meaning this..? She continued to say that you know when you guys go back home, people around will ask you about the things that you were not here to do and they will expect a good answer, because they trust that you are in the university and you should know about this. What will you say to them?

Ohm… but I did not even know. How will I know as time goes on? I understand what she was meaning to understand what other courses are dealing with, because, for example, those who are following you will ask you about the course they want to pursue, and you should be able to clarify everything to them and advise them wisely. Sometimes, we need to take lessons from those above us for us to grow because what I have learned is that they know what they are talking about. We have to know that they have gone through the process we are in, it is wise to take lessons from them just as we learn from them.

Tertiary helps us to grow in such a way that we are able to accept our responsibility in our homes, because we are studying to become something in future. We tend to look at things the other way round, that our parents have done so much for us, and it is now time to give them back what they have been giving to all of us at this time. These are the things we don't even look at when we are with our parents, but when we are without them. We see how important it is to work for what they have been doing for us in all these years. To actually create what they have been wishing to have, that is the way to thank them, isn't it good …? I wonder what you are thinking, but let's make sure you do something great for your parents or the entire family.

How does tertiary prepare us for the workplace? You might be having questions that needs answers, because you do not understand how it helps.

> ***In my own point of view, tertiary teaches us the theory that we need to apply in the workplace on how work is done, it gives us an idea of what to expect when we enter the workplace. Also, it makes us understand the areas we fall under based on the qualification a person is doing. Isn't that an idea on how tertiary is preparing us for the workplace, already we have a clear clarification about the qualification we are doing.***

Tertiary prepares us for work by providing all the information and skills that we need to know in order for us to apply all the knowledge we have at the workplace even more, because we have new strategies of solving whatever challenge we might come across. Another thing the tertiary does is to give us an overview of the interview questions on how we should go about answering them, that is also another way the tertiary is preparing us for the workplace.

Lastly, tertiary prepares us for the real world. Sometimes, lectures share their journey with students to make them understand how things are done, and how it should be done by the students in the right way after finishing studies. We learn the way from those above us because they have been through the process, we are about to go through. Tertiary prepares students for work with the time. By that I mean, they are teaching us what is relevant to how things are happening in the real, so we cannot face problems in terms of the knowledge we have about our qualification. We all know about the fourth industrial revolution that shook the world. What I can assure is that the tertiary will come up with a strategy for students to learn, what is important and will benefit them in the future.

# Final Thoughts

I asked myself how I can give lessons. What is it that I am passionate about that I can use to give others a lesson, encouragement and things they should not do or put themselves in, because even when I try to talk to people it is so easy for them to just forget about everything, and I cannot assure everyone that I want them to be a part of my talking, and they will avail themselves. These questions kept ringing in my mind. I remember myself when I was growing up, I used to write a lot. Sometimes, I think if I can get those scripts of my writing, I would have had made a huge book of them.

I realized as time goes on that I am very passionate about reading and writing, and a lot of people can see that through me. I did some searching about writing, but we are not there. What matters is that I just want to make sure, I give direction to every children out there who is about to enter the tertiary or is in the tertiary, because we come confused as to what a tertiary life in the residence may be. You may have some of your neighbors or cousins who have entered the tertiary, and they have changed in any way. So, you are wondering what is happening, am I going to end like her/him. You are afraid and your parents are fearing for you, even though it is a good thing, but they are afraid.

In the tertiary you are in control of yourself, and you chose the life that you want to live or the life that you want to create for yourself. Do not go just with the flow, look back and see where you are coming from.

This book is based on encouraging people to not forget their background when they enter the tertiary. Most of you are the hope of your families. You left behind so do not break that. I just want those who are in the tertiary with those who are about to enter the tertiary to not forget their moral and how they have been raised. In my suggestion, stick to the way you have been raised at home. You will be doing great by doing that and trust me one day you will thank yourself for doing that. You will not be having regrets and wish life can go back to fix the mistakes you have done with the opportunity you had.

I hope you take lessons and go back to re-read this book, whenever you feel like you are left out or when you consider sticking to a way you were not to be. It is very important that we respect the wishes of our parents/family. The time you show is the time when you are in the tertiary, or you are about to enter the university.

Play wisely and do not be deceived by the life, that you see now. Think about the future, because that phase is what is going to happen to you …? Change your perspective, do not just think, or take decisions for now and be sure about the decisions you are taking, and that you are not going to regret taking them in the future, and know your circle, that is my closing.

# Recommendations

## *The following is the list of the people who had a role in my writings:*

- **Mr. Romeo Matubha –DUT Riverside Librarian**

  I came to you with no direction, but an idea. You introduced me to Ms. Nelly Shozana, who is now an author. Thank you so much. You really helped me a lot, you gave me the hope that I can continue writing, when I have someone to go and ask to whenever I had a challenge.

- **Nelly Shozana- The Author**

  Thank you so much for giving me a direction on how I should go about writing the book. You made everything clear, and you gave me an opportunity to ask anything to you and that really means so much to me. Thank you.

- **Sinethemba Sijula**

  Thank you for seeing the light in me that I am actually passionate about reading and writing. Even though I knew I loved writing, but I was not starting, but you introduced me to Club Book where I got encouraged about writing. I wanted to start, it was great getting to be around people who have the same mindset. So, thank you once again.

- **Mlungisi Sibiya- Pastor**

  You always believed in me, you made me see that I was born for greatness. Thank you so much for always encouraging me to start and keep on checking, where I am with writing. You always loved every idea, I brought to you. Thank you for everything. You are indeed a true father that every child out there wishes to have.

- **Mnotho Ndlovu**

  Your support is highly appreciated and the encouragement and your wise words have throughout helped me a lot. I am grateful for that.

May be, I wouldn't have started if it wasn't for these people. I have mentioned above…., may be if I started, I would have failed through the process. I am really grateful for the effort you have put through. It is not easy writing, but when you have love and passion about it, and with the story that you want to share with the world you have to push through to make it happen.

Thank You

# References

Martin, A.J. (2012) Fear of failure in learning. In N.M. Seel (Ed). Encyclopaedia of the Sciences of Lea.

❍❍❍